Amos McGee
Misses the Bus

Erin also dedicates this book to Judy, Carolyn, Ruth Anne, Kevin, Heidi, Shelley, Karen, Megan, Portia, Morgan, Debra, Vaunda, Gail, Elsworth, and Robin.

Published by Roaring Brook Press

Roaring Brook Press is a division of Holtzbrinck Publishing Holdings Limited Partnership

120 Broadway, New York, NY 10271 • mackids.com

Library of Congress Control Number: 2021907121

ISBN 978-1-250-21322-8

Our books may be purchased in bulk for promotional, educational, or business use.
Please contact your local bookseller or the Macmillan Corporate and Premium Sales Department
at (800) 221-7945 ext. 5442 or by email at MacmillanSpecialMarkets@macmillan.com.

First edition, 2021 • Book design by Philip C. Stead and Jen Keenan
The art for this book was handmade using woodblock printing and pencil.
Printed in China by Toppan Leefung Printing Ltd., Dongguan City, Guangdong Province

1 3 5 7 9 10 8 6 4 2

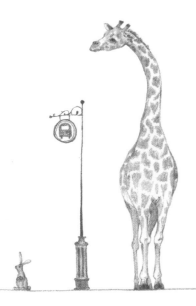

Amos McGee
Misses the Bus

Written by Philip C. Stead Illustrated by Erin E. Stead

ROARING BROOK PRESS

NEW YORK

AMOS MCGEE WAS TOO EXCITED TO SLEEP. All night long he lay awake on his pillow, planning an outing for his friends. "Of course, I'll have to finish chores early tomorrow," he said to a little mouse. "And I must remember the umbrellas."

When the alarm clock clanged, Amos lowered his groggy legs out of bed and swapped his pajamas for a fresh-pressed uniform.

Amos set a pot of water to boil, forgetting, though, to light the stove. He sat down to wait for tea and (quite accidentally) took a nap in his kitchen chair.

Beep-beep!

Amos awoke with a start. "Oh no!" he said, checking the time. "I am almost late for work!" He grabbed his boots and his favorite hat, and dashed out the door.

Beep-beep!
Amos raced as fast as his feet would carry him.

Beep-beep!
The number five bus disappeared out of sight. Amos hung his head.
"There will be no time for an outing today," he said with a sigh.
Amos began his long walk to the City Zoo.

Amos McGee arrived late for work.

"I hope you are not upset," he apologized
    to the elephant.

"It's just that I did not sleep well last night," he informed the penguin.

"And I missed the morning bus," he added to the rhinoceros.

"Which is why," he explained to the owl, "I have lost my favorite hat."

Amos yawned. "By the way," he said, sitting down a moment to rest, "has anyone seen the tortoise?"

The tortoise had stepped out for a bit of exercise.

Amos McGee had fallen asleep.
"Amos is so tired," worried the animals. "He works so hard every day."

So while Amos slept . . .

The elephant borrowed a broom and began to tidy up.
The penguin gave friendly reminders not to wake the zookeeper.
The rhinoceros made sure all the littlest creatures were fed.
The owl instructed visitors on the importance of animal conservation . . .

And the tortoise . . .

discovered a missing thing . . .

to bring to the lost and found.

And so they did.

Amos looked around and saw that his chores were done. "Thank you," he said to his friends. "There can be so many nice surprises in a day." He pulled the watch from his pocket and smiled. "If we hurry, there is even time to catch the afternoon bus."

"Hooray! My favorite hat!"

And they didn't get off until the very last stop.

Beep-beep!